A Mouse Called
Miika

NEWHAM LIBRARIES

90800101197311

Also by Matt Haig

Shadow Forest
The Runaway Troll
To Be a Cat
Echo Boy
A Boy Called Christmas
The Girl Who Saved Christmas
Father Christmas and Me
The Truth Pixie
Evie and the Animals
The Truth Pixie Goes to School
Evie in the Jungle

A Mouse Called Miika

Matt Haig

with illustrations by

Chris Mould

CANONGATE

This paperback edition first published in Great Britain
in 2022 by Canongate Books

First published in Great Britain in 2021 by Canongate Books Ltd,
14 High Street, Edinburgh EH1 1TE

canongate.co.uk

1

Copyright © Matt Haig, 2021
Illustrations copyright © Chris Mould, 2021
Extract from *A Boy Called Christmas* © Matt Haig, 2015
Illustrations copyright for *A Boy Called Christmas* © Chris Mould, 2015

The right of Matt Haig and Chris Mould to be identified as the
author and illustrator of this work has been asserted by them
in accordance with the Copyright, Designs and Patents Act 1988

British Library Cataloguing-in-Publication Data
A catalogue record for this book is available on
request from the British Library

ISBN 978 1 83885 369 3

Typeset in Bembo by Palimpsest Book Production Ltd,
Falkirk, Stirlingshire

Printed and bound in Great Britain by Clays Ltd, Elcograf S.p.A.

MIX
Paper from
responsible sources
FSC® C018072
www.fsc.org

Trolls & Elves

Loka

Owl

Nikolas

Blitzen

Father Topo

Noosh

Miika

Bridget

Truth Pixie

little Kip

Thud

A Tale of Two Mice

Two mice were sitting in a forest, leaning against a pine cone.

They were friends. And they looked quite ordinary. They had ordinary dark eyes, ordinary pink noses, ordinary tails.

Where they lived, though, was quite *un*-ordinary. Because where they lived was the Far North.

At the very top of a country that humans call Finland is a little town called Elfhelm, which is the most unique place on the whole planet. A place you won't find on any map. A place full of brightly coloured wooden houses in winding streets. A place full of elves, and flying reindeer, and the occasional pixie.

One of the mice was called Miika. He was the less scruffy of the two, but still a little bit scruffy. His brown fur was often dotted with mushroom crumbs on his chest and tummy. Unlike his friend, Miika liked the elves, the reindeer and the pixies of Elfhelm.

'I'm glad I found you,' he said, gazing through the snow-dusted trees.

'And why is that, Miika?' sighed the mouse with mud on her fur and frost on her whiskers, as if she'd heard the words many times before. The one whose name was Bridget the Brave. Well, really she was just called Bridget, but she always made Miika (and everyone else) call her Bridget the Brave. Because she was that sort of mouse. A mouse with attitude.

'Because I don't feel alone any more. I have found someone who is just like me.'

Bridget the Brave laughed. She looked past the tall pines, down towards the colourful wooden houses of the elf village that she hated so much. 'You're not like me, Miika.'

'Why not?'

'Well,' she said, 'I am Bridget the Brave. I am fearless. You are not. That's one difference.'

Miika wanted to ask in what other ways they were different. But he was too scared. So he just sat there, staring at the mushroom in front of him, and remembered his early life, when he lived in a dark and damp tree hole . . .

The Mouse with No Name

he first thing you should know about Miika is that he wasn't always called Miika.

When he was very little, he had no name at all.

It wasn't because mice don't give each other names. Because they do. *Of course* they do. It was just that normally parents give baby mice their names when they are born, and the trouble with Miika's parents was that they didn't actually know he existed.

The reason his dad – Munch – didn't know Miika existed was because when Miika was born, Munch was being eaten by a great grey owl. And it was hard to be a good parent when you were busy being digested.

His mum – Ulla – had less of an excuse

because she was, at least, alive. But she was very, very, *very* tired.

And the reason she was very, very, *very* tired was because Miika wasn't her only little mouse.

In fact, Miika was one of many little mice.

He was the thirteenth – and last – of the litter.

And though Ulla named the other twelve offspring who arrived that night, she had fallen fast asleep by the time she got to Miika.

When she woke up, Miika was just one of one hundred and nine mice she had given birth to that year in a total of eleven litters. While some of those other babies were already brown and furry, unlike the pink and hairless gang of newborns, she still found it difficult to keep up with them all. And so, she didn't bother, and Miika spent his first few days and weeks believing he was called 'That One' or 'Him Over There' or 'Please Get Off' or 'Your Bum Is In My Face'.

And Miika spent those early days very hungry indeed. He was the weakest, smallest, youngest, most ignored and unfed mouse in the whole crowded, dark, damp tree hole, and probably had the rumbliest tummy in the entire universe.

But one day, something happened.

Ulla returned with a special find.

'This,' she told all the little mice as they gathered round, 'is something really quite exciting. It is a whole button mushroom. The best in the whole forest. Since we've all eaten today already, we'll all go to sleep now and have it for breakfast tomorrow.'

But Miika thought, *Hang on a minute. I haven't eaten today.*

And he remembered the last time his mum brought home a mushroom for breakfast.

He had been pushed aside and squashed and squished and squeezed and in the end had been left with only the tiniest of crumbs.

So, this time, he decided to do something different.

That night, when all his brothers and sisters were sound asleep, he quietly crept over to his snoring mum and stared at the mushroom she was hugging in her sleep.

His stomach rumbled.

He stared and he stared and he stared.

And he knew that if he waited until morning, he wouldn't get a bite of the mushroom. And it looked *so* tasty.

So, he did something terrible.

He gently tugged the mushroom out of his mum's arms and had a tiny nibble.

And then he had another nibble.

And another.

And another.

And he kept nibbling until the whole mushroom was gone.

And then he tiptoed far away and lay down and fell asleep. It was the best sleep he had ever had in his whole short life because it was the only time he'd had a full tummy. And there is no sleep as good as a full-tummy sleep.

And he stayed fast asleep all night until a scream pulled him out of happy dreams. 'WHO STOLE THE MUSHROOM?' Ulla roared at her drowsy litter. Well, maybe not a *roar*. When a mouse roars it is only loud if you happen to be a mouse. Anyone else would just hear the tiniest of tiny squeaks.

But to Miika it was a roar and he felt so scared he shook like a leaf in the breeze and said nothing.

He said nothing all day. And he said nothing all night.

He was so scared he would get found out that he felt sick. He needed to escape. But where could he go?

That night he overheard his sister Yala talking to one of his brothers about something called The World Outside.

'The World Outside is a very dangerous place full of deadly creatures called *crows* and *owls* and *hawks* and *humans*. But it also contains food. *Mushrooms* and *insects* and something *wonderful* known as *cheese*.' Miika's ears pricked up at the sound of *cheese*, but he pretended to be asleep. He knew they wouldn't want him to join in if they saw him listening, so he stayed very still, curled up on a muddy leaf, and listened in the damp and the dark as Yala continued to offer her advice. Her shiny black eyes were wide open and her tail was flicking with excitement, in time with every word.

'In this world, little brother, it is best to care only about yourself. As soon as you start caring about others, you have to deal with all sorts of problems. So, head for the cheese whenever you can. If you find enough cheese to live on, you will never – and I repeat NEVER – want for anything else. That is as good as life gets.'

Miika felt the message was just for him. He couldn't sleep. He knew what he had to do.

In the early hours of the next morning, Miika scrambled over a hundred sleeping mice.

'Sorry . . . sorry . . . sorry . . . oh . . . so sorry!' he said, as everyone tutted and squeaked and grumbled and ouched at him.

And then he reached it.

The glowing, glorious, *terrifying* light.

The entrance to the tree hole.

He peeked out and saw blue sky and frosted grass.

It was the scariest and most beautiful thing he had ever seen.

But he would do it. He would leave the tree hole.

The outside seemed less scary than being found out as the mushroom thief. He would go into The World Outside with nothing at all.

Just himself.

(And his guilty secret.)

Miika looked back at all his brothers and all his sisters.

'Well, bye, everyone. I am going to go into The World Outside.'

But of course no one was listening. His words fell unnoticed, like snow thawing to rain before it hits the ground.

'Bye, Mum,' he said, trying to keep the sadness from his voice. 'I'm scared . . .'

But Ulla just rolled over in her sleep. And Miika left the darkness and the damp and his sleeping siblings and headed out into the world.

Out in the World

or days and weeks after leaving the tree hole, he spent every night shivering from cold and fear, never finding enough mushrooms to eat, sleeping under soggy leaves and dreaming of having a full tummy.

Then one day he found a little house in the woods. A human house. Where a woodcutter lived with his son Nikolas.

There he found comfort and a warm fire. Nikolas became his friend and taught him how to speak human words. And it was there that Nikolas gave him his name – Miika.

When Nikolas's father failed to return home from one of his voyages, Nikolas took Miika on a perilous journey to find him. They shared a big adventure to the

Far North. And Miika felt like they were the best friends in the whole world.

After that, they decided to stay in Elfhelm with the elves. Miika didn't meet any other mice there for many years, but he learned all about magic spells (or drimwicks, as the elves called them), about pixies who could only tell the truth and, best of all, about elf cheese.

But it was a joy when Miika found another mouse to hang out with. Bridget the Brave lived in a tree with a messy hoard of mushrooms and stolen cheese. And unlike Miika she wanted nothing to do with the other creatures of the Far North.

Not even the reindeer.

A Mouse, a Human and
a Reindeer

So, that brings us to right now. Where we started. The day that Miika and Bridget the Brave were leaning against the pine cone.

After they shared a mushroom, Miika left Bridget the Brave and walked back through the snowy forest of the Wooded Hills, down to Elfhelm. On the way, he bumped into an elf called Loka, who said hello and gave him a large crumb of cheese.

An hour later, Miika was still nibbling on that delicious elf cheese as he rested against the big, brown, furry belly of his favourite reindeer of all, Blitzen.

'I think this is the best cheese Loka has ever made,' he told Blitzen. 'She is so kind. She deserves better than Moodon. I mean,

I know he's *nice* – you know, in that elf way – but she should never have married him.' Miika sighed. 'I'm not saying she should have married me. I mean, that would have been weird. A mouse and an elf probably wouldn't have worked out. But *Moodon*? He's such a mudfungle.'

Mudfungle was a word that Miika had learned from his housemate the Truth Pixie. He didn't know what it meant but he knew it was incredibly rude because he had asked the Truth Pixie to say the rudest word she could think of and she had said mudfungle. And she was the Truth Pixie after all, so she couldn't lie.

Blitzen said nothing. Blitzen never said *anything*. Blitzen just lay there in the snow of Reindeer Field, watching his reindeer friends chasing each other around in the air above and (possibly) wishing the mouse would leave him alone.

Miika heard voices and turned to see Nikolas walking briskly across the field, making boot prints in the snow. His head was bowed and he was busy talking to some elves from the workshop.

'Hi!' said Miika. 'Woo-hoo!' He tried calling the boy's name. 'Nikolas! Nikolas!' And then he tried his nickname – the name Nikolas's mum used to call him. 'Christmas! Over here! It's me – Miika!'

'Oh, hi, Miika,' said the boy, smiling as he kept on walking. 'Sorry. We're in a bit of a rush. I'd love to stop and chat, but there's an Elf Council meeting in two minutes. It's quite urgent. It's about gingerbread supplies. See you later!'

Miika smiled back, trying to hide his sadness. 'Okay, yeah, fine. Totally. See you later . . . I'm just hanging out with Blitzen. You know, buddy to buddy. We're having a great time.' But deep inside he wished Nikolas had more time for him, like in the old days. But Nikolas – the only human for miles around – was so popular with the elves he always had some important thing to do. *He's not even an elf*, Miika thought to himself grumpily. He cheered himself by remembering that he didn't really need Nikolas because most afternoons he spent his time with another friend – Bridget the Brave, his mischievous companion.

But then he remembered what Bridget had said earlier. About him lacking courage. Maybe he did need to work on being fearless. Like Bridget the Brave.

'Yes,' he said to himself. 'Brave.'

Miika turned to the reindeer. 'Blitzen, I have an idea. Can we fly, Blitzen? What do you think? Just to get me home?'

Blitzen yawned and gave Miika a frowning kind of look.

Miika knew he was pushing his luck. 'Please, Blitzen! Come on, big guy. It'll be fun. I'll just hold on to your neck.'

Blitzen didn't move.

'Look, it's nearly dark now. And it's getting cold. It's a long way for me to walk back to the Truth Pixie's house. You could fly me there!'

Blitzen sighed again. But this was a

different sigh. It was an *okay then, climb on, you annoying little mouse*-type of sigh. So, Miika grabbed on to the warm reindeer's belly hair and climbed up onto his back as Blitzen got to his feet.

'Thanks, Blitzen,' said the mouse.

And then they were off. Galloping across the snowy field, which even in the middle of summer was as white and fluffy as a beard.

Then came Miika's favourite part. The magic part. He listened very hard to hear it. Or rather, *not* hear it. The moment Blitzen's hooves stopped pounding against the ground and trod silently against the cold north air itself.

Up and up, against the laws of gravity, and into the sky.

Flying

s they soared over Elfhelm, over
the frozen Mirror Lake, above
the snow-garnished roofs of elf
houses and shops that lined
the Street of Seven Curves,
Miika was feeling brave. Very brave. Wait
until Bridget the Brave heard about this,
he thought. But he couldn't help feeling
he could be even braver.'

And so, as the wind picked up and ruffled
his mouse fur, he crawled up towards the
reindeer's neck, and kept going.

Blitzen turned his head and gave the
mouse a cross look.

'It'll be fine, big guy,' Miika said. 'I
promise. I've just got to do this.'

And it *was* fine. For a little while. Miika
scurried right up to the top of Blitzen's head
and then even further – up his right antler,

to the very tip. He balanced there on his hind legs, feeling the rush of cold wind.

'Wooooh-hoooh! Antler surfing!'

Miika gazed down at the glowing windows of Elfhelm, and then across to the forest. He hoped that Bridget the Brave was out of her mouse hole, watching his fearlessness.

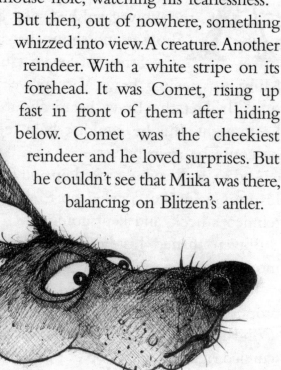

But then, out of nowhere, something whizzed into view. A creature. Another reindeer. With a white stripe on its forehead. It was Comet, rising up fast in front of them after hiding below. Comet was the cheekiest reindeer and he loved surprises. But he couldn't see that Miika was there, balancing on Blitzen's antler.

Blitzen's head shot back in surprise.

'Aaaaaahhhhhh!' screamed Miika as he tried to keep hold of Blitzen. But it was too late.

He was falling through the air, tumbling and tumbling, faster and faster. Blitzen desperately tried to see his little friend but he was already lost in the darkness of the night sky.

EeeeeeeeekKKKKK

The Untasted Cheese

As he tossed and turned through the air, Miika remembered Bridget the Brave telling him about the most amazing and special cheese she had ever tasted.

'The most amazing and special cheese I ever tasted,' she had said, 'was a cheese called Urga-burga cheese. It is the greatest and stinkiest cheese in the whole universe. It is a mouldy blue colour, like a clear sky, and it doesn't just taste brilliant, it makes you *feel* brilliant. One taste and you're happy for days. It's amazing! I've only tasted it once. But I hope I'll taste it again one day . . .'

And Miika realised he was going to die without ever having tasted Urga-burga cheese.

Landing

It wasn't the falling that was the problem.

It was the *landing*.

His body landed with a crunch on the snowy roof of one of the elf houses and then bounced off the tiles to the street below, amidst the usual evening sounds of chatter and the scent of gingerbread.

Miika felt as if his body had been taken apart and every little mouse bone put back together again in the wrong order.

Even though the street was packed with busy elves, no one noticed Miika fall to the ground. Well, no one except an elf girl with wide eyes and sharp cheeks, who was staring at him through a window in the house across the street.

He recognised this girl. It was Noosh.
A moment later, and she was rushing out of her house through the snow towards him, but Miika couldn't see her any more. Everything had gone very dark.

In the Truth Pixie's Cottage

aybe I'm dead, thought Miika. *But if I'm thinking I'm dead, I'm probably not dead. I'm pretty sure thinking is a thing you need to be alive to do.*

Then he noticed something.

All the pain had gone.

His banged-up body that had crunched so hard against the roof and then onto the street felt totally normal. In fact, if anything, Miika felt *better* than normal. It felt as though his whole body was being filled from the inside with a warm syrup. And there was a familiar but delicious smell in the air.

He opened his eyes.

And he realised he wasn't out in the street any more. He was in the cosy little cottage where he lived with the Truth Pixie.

And there was the Truth Pixie herself, right in front of him, holding a large crumb of cheese to his nose. Miika gobbled it in one go.

'What happened?' he said.

The Truth Pixie shrugged. 'I was sitting in the rocking chair, just reading a little bit. It was lovely and relaxing. The book I'm reading is that one over there. It's called *The Really Stupid Trolls Who Exploded*. It's very good. So clever. So many *layers*. Quite emotional. It reminds me of the hilarious time I gave a troll a hewlip leaf and made his head explode. I can't wait to discuss it at the Pixie Book Club. Even though I'm the only member of the Pixie Book Club, so it will just be me talking to myself. Which, I suppose, now that I come to think about it, I could do any time I want, really.'

Miika shook his head. 'I mean what happened *to me*?'

The Truth Pixie gasped and slapped her face as if she had only just thought about it. 'Oh – *to you*! Um, I don't know actually. Noosh carried you here and said you'd had a bit of a fall. But you seem perfectly fine now.'

'*A bit of a fall!* I fell out of the sky!'

'The sky? What were you doing in the sky?'

'I, um, well . . . I was riding Blitzen. He was bringing me home. And, yeah, I slipped off his antler, and I landed on a roof, and it was really painful, and I felt like I was dying . . . but now I feel . . . fine. Better than fine.'

The Truth Pixie gasped again. And then smiled. And then giggled. And she kept giggling for what seemed like an hour.

'What's so funny?' said Miika eventually.

'I've just realised what's happened to you!' the Truth Pixie said eventually, calming herself down.

'What?' Miika asked, his nose twitching with worry.

'Don't you know?'

'Know *what*?'

The Truth Pixie leaned in really close and whispered as if telling him the world's biggest secret. 'I think, my little mouse friend, that you've been drimwicked.'

t was true.

Miika asked the Truth Pixie to take him urgently to visit Noosh and Father Topo in their house on the Street of Seven Curves.

'One moment,' said the Truth Pixie, pointing at her book. 'I just have one sentence left. You can never leave a story with just one sentence left. It's very bad luck. I once knew someone who stopped reading a story right near the end.'

'What happened?'

'She died. I mean, it was seventeen years later. But you can't be too careful.'

And so she finished reading *The Really Stupid Trolls Who Exploded*, wiped the tears from her eyes, put Miika in her pocket and ran down the hill to Elfhelm.

Once inside the elves' house, with its sloping floor and crooked cupboards, things became clear.

Noosh, having found Miika lying on the street, had picked him up and had indeed cast a hope spell – a drimwick – and it had obviously worked because he stayed alive. And now he was pain-free! And Noosh was very excited about this because it was the first time she had ever performed a drimwick, but her great-great-great-great-great-grandpa wasn't quite so impressed.

'Now, Noosh, I have told you many times,' said Father Topo, stroking his beard. 'You should never attempt a drimwick without supervision. It says so in the first *Book of Hope & Wonder*.'

'But you weren't there! And Miika was in danger. I had to do something! I only put my hands around him and wished him to be warm, and strong, and always safe . . . I drimwicked him! I didn't think I could because I know how hard drimwickery is – and I didn't know if I had enough hope inside me – but I suppose because he is a mouse, he was small enough for it to work.'

'So, I *am* drimwicked,' Miika muttered.

'Yes. You've received a hope spell,' explained Father Topo. 'Like the one I gave Nikolas. A drimwick is one of the very first spells in elf magic.'

'It means that you are now part-mouse and part-magic,' explained Noosh, who was playing with a spinning top. 'In the way that Nikolas is part-human and part-magic. It's all *very* exciting!'

Father Topo sighed as he checked on the gingerbread elves he was baking in the oven. 'It is *not* exciting, Noosh. It is deeply *worrying.*There has never been a drimwicked mouse before.'

'What could go wrong?' asked Miika, in a voice that would have been pale and milky if voices could have colours.

It was at this point that the Truth Pixie joined the conversation. 'All kinds of things,' she said. 'For instance, once there was a bear who was drimwicked, and she went quite mad. She spent entire days talking to snow and eating reindeer poo. It was very sad.'

'Crikey,' said Miika. 'That doesn't sound fun.'

'Now, now, Truth Pixie,' said Father Topo, taking the gingerbread out of the oven. 'That was a very long time ago. And a most unusual case.'

'So, what do you think will happen to me?' Miika asked the wise old elf.

Father Topo placed the gingerbread elves on a tray and offered them to everyone.

He even broke off a little bit and gave it to Miika. Gingerbread might not have been as tasty as cheese, but it was a million times better than mushrooms and Miika was always grateful for it.

'What I think will happen to you,' said Father Topo. 'Hmmm . . . Well, I think that rather depends on you.'

'On me? Oh no.'

Father Topo nodded. 'Yes. You see, a drimwick basically brings out the qualities that you already have. Your potential. It means you will get a chance to find out who you really are. A drimwick gives different people different powers, but one thing is for sure, little Miika, your life will never be the same again.'

A Mouse Called Bridget the Brave

Bridget the Brave was the only other mouse Miika had met since arriving in the Far North. He had met her on a day when he was feeling particularly lonely, as Nikolas had been helping to organise the Elfhelm snowball contest and the Truth Pixie had been writing a book of poetry.

That was a few months ago.

And now they were good friends. Miika knew this, because he had asked her about seventy-two times.

'It does feel good,' thought Miika aloud, right now, 'to have a friend of the same species. Hey, on that subject . . . do you know why there are so few mice around here?'

According to Bridget the Brave, there

were other mice but most had found it too cold in the Far North and had headed south. Or they had been eaten by a snowy owl called Snow Owl.

'Gulp,' gulped Miika.

'Exactly,' said Bridget the Brave. 'But I haven't seen any trace of Snow Owl for a long time, and to be honest, the fewer mice there are, the more food there is for us.'

They were walking through the Wooded Hills, on a snowless and well-trodden path, looking for mushrooms.

'That's true, Bridget the Brave. But don't you ever get bored of mushrooms?'

Bridget the Brave stopped and sighed the longest sigh in the whole of mouse history. 'Of course. I am totally, totally bored of mushrooms. But I'm not like you. I don't have all your elf contacts. I can't just go up to an elf and do a cute little face and get them to give me cheese! In fact, every time I go into Elfhelm they chase me away.'

Miika looked at his friend. She seemed

muddier and scruffier and wilder than ever. He couldn't help but feel a little bit annoyed at this.

'Well,' said Miika, 'it's not my fault that you, um, tried to rob the Elfhelm Cheese Shop.'

Bridget the Brave tutted. '*Tried!* There was no *tried*. I *successfully* robbed the Elfhelm Cheese Shop. It's just that they caught me. Stupid, do-goody elves!'

Miika didn't like it when Bridget the Brave talked like this. And she talked like this quite a lot, but what he hated even more was the thought of losing her as a friend.

'Yeah,' said Miika, trying to impress her. 'Do-goody elves.'

But then up ahead he saw someone.

'We should probably be quiet,' said Miika, pointing at an elf boy in a blue tunic crouched amid the trees, picking up pine cones. 'As quiet as mice. Because, you know, elves have feelings too!'

'He can't hear me. And I don't care.'

'Elves actually have very good hearing.

And understand ninety per cent of animals, including mice. Isn't that right, Kip?'

The elf boy turned around at the sound of his name, as he placed another pine cone in his basket. He smiled. And nodded. And said nothing, just carried on collecting cones.

Miika realised the wind had blown cold, because Bridget the Brave was now shivering.

'S-s-such a w-w-weirdo,' whispered Bridget the Brave, stuttering with cold.

'He's actually been through quite a lot,' Miika told her.

'And? Why would you care?'

'I don't,' pretended Miika. 'Not at all.'

Bridget the Brave spotted a bright-green mushroom near a hewlip bush and scurried

towards it. Miika followed and sat next to her amid the snow-dusted leaves.

'It's s-s-s-s-s-so c-c-c-c-c-cold today,' said Bridget the Brave melodramatically.

'Is it?' said Miika, who felt perfectly warm.

'Yes! It's f-f-f-f-f-freezing. It's the coldest day of summer.'

Miika quickly nodded. He wondered if it was because he had been drimwicked that he wasn't feeling the cold weather. 'Yes,' he lied. 'Actually, now you mention it, it really is quite cold, isn't it?'

'So,' said Bridget the Brave, with her mouth full of fungus, 'what have you been up to, Miika? There seems to be something different about you.'

Miika felt worried. He didn't want to tell his friend about having been drimwicked. It was bad enough – in Bridget the Brave's eyes – that Miika lived with a pixie and knew elves and was friends with a human. If he told her that he was now drimwicked and had magical powers and could maybe live for ever then

Miika doubted that she would still want to be friends with him.

'Oooh,' said Miika. 'What have I been up to? That's a good question. What have I been up to? What have I been up to? What *have* I been up to? Not much, really . . . Just, you know, sitting. And sleeping. And existing. And trying to keep out of the cold. It's been a very normal time. Totally normal. Normal to the power of normal.'

And in a way, Miika supposed, this wasn't really a lie. Or not a *big* lie anyway.

You see, despite the fall and the near-death experience and the drimwick nothing really *had* changed. If Miika did have magical powers, he hadn't discovered them. Except, well, he really did feel warm and Bridget the Brave really didn't, so maybe that was all that had happened.

She suddenly stopped chewing on her mushroom. 'Oh no,' she said.

'Oh what?' wondered Miika.

'Oh *look*!'

Miika looked to where she was pointing

and saw it. A large black ball in the snow, a short distance into the trees.

Bridget the Brave rushed over to inspect it, with Miika close behind.

'You know what this is, don't you?' Bridget the Brave asked.

'What?'

'It is deadly danger, that's what.'

It didn't exactly look like deadly danger, thought Miika. It looked like a big ball of black mud. But then Miika noticed something sticking out of it. Something hard and bone-white. A small skull. A delicate skull. A *mouse skull*.

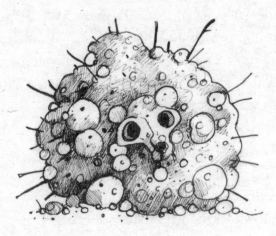

Bridget the Brave looked up to the sky nervously. 'You see, Miika, this ball of dirt isn't just any old ball of dirt. This is an owl pellet. And you know what an owl pellet is, don't you?'

'What?' said Miika in his pale voice.

'It's the most disgusting thing in the whole of nature. Coughed up by owls. All the things their stomach can't handle. All the fur and the hair and the bones. And l-l-look at the colour. It's totally black. That means it's fresh. Which means Snow Owl must be around here, somewhere. She's probably watching us right now.'

iika gulped.

He had always thought the terrifying stories of Snow Owl weren't true, because Bridget the Brave had a habit of exaggerating and making things up. Like the time she said she had made a brown bear run away by giving him a really cross look. But there was no arguing with a giant ball of regurgitated undigested mouse!

As he turned away from the monstrous sight, he saw something even worse.

Sitting on the branch above them was something frost-white and oval and feathery, speckled with tiny black markings. Something with large, yellow unmoving eyes staring straight at them. Something pristine and beautiful and terrifying.

'She's there,' whispered Miika. 'It's Snow Owl.'

'*Run!*' squealed Bridget the Brave – or, in that moment, Bridget the Not So Brave.

And the two frightened mice watched in horror as the owl lifted up her vast wings and swooped into the air, straight towards them.

Big Trouble

Even the fastest mouse in the world can't run faster than an owl can fly. And neither Miika nor Bridget the Brave were the fastest mouse in the world.

They were a long way from Bridget the Brave's tree hole and there were no other tree holes in sight. They froze with fear.

'We're going to die!' said Bridget the Not So Brave.

It was hard to argue, when a giant snowy owl was swooping down towards them. And unlike reindeers, owls were pretty easy to understand.

'I can see yooooooou,' screeched Snow Owl. 'And sooooooon I will taste yooooooou. Yooooooou can't escape. But doooooo run. I like a warm lunch, I doooooo.'

The two mice started to run, but it was really hard to run in deep snow. And then Bridget the Brave got one of her feet caught under a twig.

'Miika! *My best friend in the whole world!* Save me! Help get this twig off me! Please! I'm scared!'

'I'm coming,' said Miika, scampering back towards his friend.

But it was too late.

Snow Owl was inches off the ground, just above Bridget the Brave. 'Ta-wit-ta-woooooo, how do you dooooooo?'

Miika stared at the owl and for a moment did nothing except wish. He wished harder than he had ever wished in his life. And what he wished was for the owl to GO AWAY.

As he wished he felt his whole body grow strong, and he had that warm syrupy feeling again. And just as the owl's clawed feet were about to sink into his friend, Miika found himself staring harder than he had ever stared in his life. As he stared at the owl, he felt the whole world disappear. In that moment, there was only him and the owl and one single hope – for the creature to go away.

Then the most remarkable thing happened.

A sudden blast of bright golden light appeared immediately in front of the owl, like a tiny little sun, and this tiny little sun pressed into Snow Owl's chest, and she shot backwards as if hit by a cannonball. As Miika kept staring, he realised he was the one with this power. The power to move Snow Owl. After the owl shot back in mid-air, Miika held her in one spot, a little distance away, high above Bridget the Brave, hovering like a feathered sculpture.

'Leave us alone,' Miika said, with his voice but mainly his mind. 'Don't ever try to hurt us again. Or my magic will finish you. Do you understand?'

The terrified owl was clearly in a state of shock. 'I doooooo.'

'Good. Now go. Fly away and don't come back. And if you haven't disappeared out of sight after I count to ten, you're in BIG TROUBLE.'

Miika let the bird free, with his mind, and the owl flew away faster than a blizzard wind.

An Impossibility

ridget the Brave could hardly speak. Her mouth opened and closed and opened and closed and opened again. 'What . . . did . . . you . . . do?'

'I think I might have saved your life. No big deal.'

'Miika! You just made light appear out of thin air! How? What? *How?* That was impossible!'

And Miika remembered something he had once heard the wise old elf Father Topo say . . .

'An impossibility is just a possibility you don't understand yet'

They scurried back to Bridget the Brave's tree hole, passing Kip and his basket full of pine cones, and Miika began to explain everything to his friend.

An Argument

o, I suppose you think you're brave now, don't you? Brave and special.'

They were back inside the tree hole, sitting on a small pile of damp leaves in the dark, and Bridget the Brave was in a huff, her tiny crossed arms matching the frown on her face.

'Don't be like that. I didn't ask to be drimwicked.'

'Being an ordinary mouse was never good enough for you, was it?'

Miika shook his head. He had just saved Bridget the Brave's life and, for once, he decided to say what he really felt. 'You sound jealous.'

'No, Miika, I'm not jealous. Because, unlike you, I'm not ashamed of who I am. I am a mouse. A fearless and brave mouse.'

'I'm not ashamed,' said Miika.

'Hmmm,' said Bridget the Brave, scratching her belly. 'I think you have a problem with being a mouse.'

'No, I don't.'

'Think about it. You left your family behind—'

'My family didn't want me! My mum didn't even give me a name!'

Bridget the Brave ignored Miika's protests. 'Then you went and became best friends with a human . . .'

'And?'

'Now you live with a pixie . . .'

'So?'

'And you *wanted* to be drimwicked!'

Bridget the Brave said drimwicked as if it was a swear word. 'I DID NOT WANT TO BE DRIM-WICKED. I DID NOT ASK TO BE

DRIMWICKED. I DID NOT PLAN TO BE DRIMWICKED! AND I JUST SAVED YOUR LIFE!'

'No, you didn't. I had the situation entirely under control.'

'That isn't true, Bridget, and you know it.'

'Bridget *the Brave* – that's my name.'

'Sorry, Bridget the Brave. But you wanted my help. You said you were scared.'

And with those words his companion's eyes widened with rage. 'Liar! I never said that! How could *I* – Bridget the Brave – ever say such a thing!'

'I'm sorry. Maybe I misheard.'

And Bridget the Brave scowled some more. It was the scowliest scowl Miika had ever seen. 'The truth is, Miika, whether you planned it or not, you were drimwicked because you fell off your silly reindeer friend, Blister.'

'Blitzen.'

'What?'

'He's, um, called Blitzen.'

'Yeah. That's what I said. Blister. And it also only happened because the elf girl knew you . . .'

'Wow,' whispered Miika. 'You really are jealous, aren't you?'

Bridget the Brave burped a mushroomy burp. 'Why would I be jealous of a mouse who doesn't really want to be a mouse? You see, Miika, I know what I am. I am a mouse.'

'Same here.'

'No. Not really. I *want* to be a mouse. And I *am* a mouse. A wild and free forest mouse, living in my tree hole, eating mushrooms and sleeping on a bed of leaves. Meanwhile you live in that weird yellow cottage, eating gingerbread crumbs and sleeping on a comfy rug by the fire and spending the whole year looking forward to Christmas. It's really very, very sad. You are a traitor to mice. And, quite frankly, I don't think we can be friends any more.'

'*What?!*'

But Bridget the Brave was adamant, and

she stood up and went over to the bright entrance of the tree hole. She pointed out at the snow and fallen pine cones. 'Go on. Get out. Go and be with the magic creatures. You clearly prefer them to *mice.*'

Miika felt as though he might cry, and he had never cried in his life.

'This is ridiculous. Please, Bridget . . . the Brave. This is silly.'

But Bridget the Brave shook her head and pointed out towards the snow again.

'Fine,' Miika said. And he kept on saying it as he left and went back into the cold, even when Bridget the Brave couldn't hear him any more. He kept saying the word as he walked, through the snow and the giant pines and silver birches, all the way back to the Truth Pixie's cottage.

'Fine,' he said, trying not to think about the warm wet feeling in his eyes and the sad heavy feeling in his body. 'Fine. Fine. Fine . . . *Fine.*'

A Life of Infinite Loneliness and Crushing Disappointment

The Truth Pixie was busy writing a list of her least favourite pixies of all time, and Miika was lying on his rug by the warmth of the fire.

'The Grump Pixie . . .' muttered the pixie. 'He is number thirty-seven. The Awkward Stare Pixie. Definitely number thirty-six . . .'

Then she looked up and saw Miika and the sadness of his droopy ears. 'What's the matter with you?' she asked.

'It's a long story. I don't want to bore you with it.'

'Well, that's good. Because I don't want to be bored.' And the Truth Pixie carried on with her list. 'Number thirty-five. The Incessant Humming Pixie . . .'

Miika decided to act as if the Truth Pixie *was* interested. 'I had only one mouse friend. And now I don't even have her any more. She thinks that now I'm drimwicked, it's proof I don't want to be a mouse.'

'Well,' sighed the Truth Pixie, 'to be fair, you don't act like a mouse.'

'What?' said Miika, sitting up.

'Look at you. You're on a rug. By the fire. You're practically a cat.'

'That is a *disgusting* thing to say, Truth Pixie.'

The Truth Pixie shrugged. 'The truth is all I have.'

Miika groaned. 'I just feel like I'll never fit anywhere. I'm not an elf. I'm not a human. I'm not a pixie. And I'm not even a mouse. Not a proper one . . .'

The Truth Pixie nodded, without looking up from her list. 'You're probably right. A life of infinite loneliness and crushing disappointment may await you.'

'Great,' grumbled Miika.

'But I'm the same,' said the Truth Pixie.

'No one likes me either. Well, apart from Nikolas, but he doesn't count because he likes everyone. Even you. And at least me and you have each other to talk to. I mean, don't get me wrong, you can be *very* annoying, but at least you're *there*. And that means a lot sometimes. Having somebody who's there.'

Miika forced a little smile. 'Um, thanks . . . I think.'

The Truth Pixie stopped writing her list for a moment and looked up from her little table. 'The truth is, you'll never be happy with yourself if you spend your life worrying what people think of you. And I should know. Every pixie in the entire world thinks I'm awful because I tell the truth. And pixies don't really like the truth. It gives them a rash. Sometimes, if they're flying pixies, it even makes their wings fall off.'

'Wow. I didn't know that.'

'Well, I can't lie, so believe it. I didn't *ask* to be like this. I didn't *ask* to be a Truth

Pixie. I didn't ask for my aunt to cast a spell when I was little that meant I would have to tell the truth for ever. We don't ask to be who we are. But when we *are* who we are there's very little point hating who we are. Because who we are is WHO WE ARE. Understand?'

'I think so,' said Miika.

And he smiled and liked these words and found them soothing. But he still felt lonely inside, and although he didn't like that feeling, he didn't tell the Truth Pixie about it. He just lay back down on the rug in silence, watching the glowing fire and sighing now and again.

A White-Spotted Love Button Mushroom

The next day, Miika went out searching for mushrooms, but it felt strange having to do it all alone. He missed his friend. When he heard a familiar voice calling his name from behind a tree, his heart lifted like a flying reindeer.

'Bridget the Brave? Is that you?' Miika called back.

And it was indeed his scruffy friend. Or, *former* friend. Miika stood still as Bridget the Brave scurried around to see him. She held out a tiny green mushroom with white spots.

'I found it earlier,' she said.

'A white-spotted love button mushroom,' gasped Miika, knowing them to be the

tastiest species of mushroom in the whole
of the Far North.

'I saved it for you,' said Bridget the Brave
meekly. 'To say sorry. About yesterday. I
didn't mean what I said. I was just shocked,
you know, from Snow Owl. Even Bridget
the Brave has moments of weakness.' She
smiled at him. 'Maybe I should change my
name to Bridget the Brave Ninety-Nine
Point Nine Nine Nine Per Cent of the
Time? It's just not as catchy. And I should

have said thank you for saving my life. I was too proud. I was a bit –' she struggled to say the next word '– jealous. You were right, and I'm sorry. Will you forgive me?'

Miika took the mushroom and ate the mushroom and enjoyed the mushroom. It wasn't quite as good as cheese. But it was, without question, among the top ten mushrooms Miika had ever tasted.

'Yes!' he said. 'Of course I forgive you. But, one question: the next time an owl tries to eat you alive should I just leave them to it?'

Bridget the Brave laughed. 'Well, I suppose it's what I deserve.'

'Yes, it is. But I won't. I would save your life all over again. Just to punish you and' – he started laughing with her – 'to make you realise how awesome my powers are.'

Bridget the Brave came close to Miika. She placed a little mouse arm around her friend and whispered in his ear, 'Do you want to see something special?'

Miika counted to ten to keep her waiting – and because mice aren't great at arithmetic this took quite some time – but eventually he said, 'Sure.' Because he could never resist seeing something special.

'Then follow me.'

Bridget the Brave skipped away, leading him over the snow, past a fallen branch, and then a little further through more even snow until they reached a large tree. Or rather, the trunk of a tree. It had a few small branches sticking out of it, but mainly

it was trunk, and the top was as wide as the bottom.

Bridget the Brave pointed to a little hole that had been made by a woodpecker. 'Look inside,' she said.

So Miika did and didn't see much except darkness.

Bridget the Brave darted around the base of the trunk to a bigger-sized hole on the other side, about the size of a horseshoe.

'Look. It's *hollow*,' said Bridget the Brave. 'This is the Hollow Tree. Hollow from top to bottom. It's not a pine or a silver birch. It's not like my tree with a tiny little hole for me to live in. This tree is *all hole*. It grows exactly like this – like a giant bucket made of wood. A perfect hiding place.' She was gesturing wildly with her little arms. 'Now, I've been thinking about something. And I have a plan. A brilliant plan. Are you ready for an adventure? A brave adventure.'

Miika remembered one of Bridget the Brave's earlier plans to squeak rude insults at a passing wolverine, which nearly got them both killed.

Bridget the Brave was *full* of plans. Dangerous plans.

And Miika always went along with them, because he liked having a friend, even if he secretly knew she was dangerous. If he ever raised an objection, Bridget the Brave would call him a coward and go in a huff, so Miika agreed to all kinds of silly stuff.

And now was no different.

Miika felt happy to be back with his friend again. Having a friend was a better kind of magic than being drimwicked. Even if it was a friend like Bridget the Brave.

'Yes,' he said, trying to hide his worry. 'Of course. I'm ready for an adventure.'

'That's good,' said Bridget the Brave. 'Because I have just thought of the best adventure EVER.'

The Urga-burga Plan

'First, I have a test for you . . . Move that,' said Bridget the Brave, pointing over to the heavy-looking branch of a pine tree.

'What?' Miika's eyes bulged with worry and confusion.

'Go on, see if you can use your drimwick powers. Lift it up into the air.'

Miika stared at the snowy branch. But nothing happened. *Move*, he said in his mind. *Rise*.

It was no good. The branch stayed where it was.

'Well, that *is* disappointing,' said Bridget the Brave, with a tut.

But just at that moment Miika could feel it. That warm feeling of strength. The branch moved, just by a whisker. And

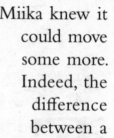

Miika knew it could move some more. Indeed, the difference between a still branch and a moving branch was infinitesimal. Once his mind had made something move a little bit, he realised he could make it move A LOT. The very next moment, the large twisted branch trembled, then lifted high into the air. The snow fell from it in thick clumps as it wobbled upwards, glowing faintly from the magical drimwickery Miika was using.

'I'm doing it. I'm doing it,' said Miika. 'Look!'

'I can see!' Bridget the Brave said, her tail wiggling in delight.

'It's actually pretty easy,' said Miika casually, as the branch floated above them.

'Now, Miika, my dear friend, you remember that troll cheese I told you about?' said Bridget the Brave excitedly, still staring at the hovering branch. 'The most amazing and special cheese I ever tasted?'

'Urga-burga cheese?' said Miika, letting the branch fall to the ground with a thud.

He remembered how Bridget the Brave had described it.

The greatest and stinkiest cheese in the whole universe . . . a mouldy blue colour, like a clear sky, and it doesn't just taste brilliant, it makes you feel brilliant. One taste and you're happy for days.

'Yes,' said Bridget the Brave, sitting down beside a pine tree. 'Urga-burga cheese. Well, as I told you, I've only tasted it once. Back when I was little and still lived with my parents. We lived right on the edge of Troll Valley, and once some of the trolls started having a massive food fight (as trolls do from time to time), and food started raining from the sky. We had never seen anything like it! Stinky troll sausage and rock bread and slime pie. One of the rock bread rolls landed on my brother, Grubber, and he died. Everyone was running as fast as they could to get back to our mouse hole for, you know, *fear of imminent death*, but then we noticed something. A *smell*. The most INCREDIBLE smell. The most wonderful, intoxicating, magical smell. The kind of smell that – even when rock bread is falling from the sky – makes you think of nothing else. And so me and my seventeen siblings followed our noses and came across this lump of entirely blue cheese. After much arguing we agreed to divide the cheese into seventeen pieces. One tiny little crumb for each of us. Oh, what a moment! I hoped I would one day taste it again . . .'

Bridget the Brave closed her eyes, remembering.

Miika felt hungry simply hearing this story, but he was also confused.

'It sounds like really good cheese. But why are you telling me this?'

Bridget the Brave's eyes sprang open. 'Because Troll Valley is still there. And it's not too far from here.'

'And?'

'And so are trolls. And so is Urga-burga cheese. And so are adventures!'

Miika shrugged. 'I'm not sure I follow. What are you suggesting, Bridget the Brave?'

'I am *suggesting* that if we start walking now, we could be at Troll Valley before nightfall.'

'But why would we want to go to Troll Valley?' asked Miika. Suddenly, he realised. 'No, Bridget the Brave. We can't go and steal some cheese from trolls. That is not going to happen. Because they are . . . *trolls*. Giant, murderous *trolls*. Trolls who would stamp on us without a second thought. Trolls whose feet are so humungous there would be no escape, no matter how fast we ran. Do you know how many mice are killed annually by trolls? Have you seen the statistics?'

'No. Have you?'

'Well, no. But that's not the point. The point is, it is *a lot*. We'd be killed.'

Bridget the Brave shook her head as if Miika was missing the point. 'But, Miika, this is the old you talking. You've been drimwicked now, remember? You made Snow Owl shoot through the air. You can lift ginormous branches. You have invincible powers. You are brave.'

'Yeah, but—'

'So, all we'd have to do is get to Troll Valley. We'll sniff out the location of the Urga-burga, then you do your magic and send the cheese flying this way.'

'But that's *stealing*. It just seems wrong.'

Bridget the Brave looked disappointed. 'Mice don't steal cheese, Miika. We take it. Because that's what mice do. That's our nature. It's the purest nature of all. A mouse taking cheese. You are still a mouse, aren't you?'

This made Miika grumpy, but also a little worried he was about to lose his friend again. 'Of course I am! But it's also in my nature to be scared by giant angry trolls who could kill us with one not-so-little finger!'

'You've been drimwicked. You aren't dying any time soon. Please, Miika. Let's do this together.'

'But what if we do it, and we're successful, and we steal – sorry, take – the cheese, and we bring it back here. What then?'

Bridget the Brave laughed. 'Then we store it in the Hollow Tree. Where no one can find it. Then we eat it. And we keep eating it. Day after day after day. And we stay happy. And we never have to hunt for a boring mushroom ever again.'

'Yeah, but—'

'Yeah but yeah but yeah but yeah but . . . I've met woodpeckers who repeat themselves less than you, Miika! If you'd tasted Urga-burga you would understand. It is a total no-brainer. Have you never had the guts to just *take* something?'

Miika remembered being a little mouse, taking the mushroom from his sleeping mother and eating it all by himself.

'Once,' mumbled Miika.

'I am going to Troll Valley with or without you ... But if you aren't going to come, don't bother being around when I get back. I don't want a coward as a friend.'

And Bridget the Brave started walking, in the opposite direction, to Troll Valley.

'But you'll be killed!'

'Well, you'd better come and look after me then, hadn't you? Are you a coward ... or a *mouse*?'

Miika sighed, and really hoped the taste of Urga-burga cheese was worth it, as he followed his friend deeper into the forest.

Troll Valley

They reached the edge of the forest, where they followed two giant four-toed footprints until they saw caves and goat skeletons and, finally, the craggy slopes of Troll Valley.

There was only one troll in sight. He was in the distance, giant and hunched and grey and lumpy, and he was lighting a fire in the middle of the valley. His shadow stretched behind him for a mile.

Miika clutched the golden hewlip leaves he had collected back in the forest.

'Why are you carrying those leaves?' Bridget the Brave asked him.

'Protection. The Truth Pixie told me that if you insert a hewlip leaf into the mouth of a troll then ten seconds later their head will explode. Here.' Miika held out a leaf. 'Have one just in case.'

Bridget the Brave took one reluctantly. 'Fine . . . Now, follow me.'

The two mice scuttled down the side of the valley, Miika following Bridget the Brave. He kept his eyes on the giant troll, sitting with his back to them, and watched as other trolls joined the fireside gathering. All of a sudden they started singing a raucous song that boomed around the valley in a kind of chant . . .

THE WORLD IS RATHER SCARY
BUT WHILE WE'RE BIG AND HAIRY
WE DON'T HAVE TO CARE-Y
DON'T NEED NO ELF OR FAIRY
OR STUPID BOOKS IN LIBRARY
BECAUSE WE HAVE A DAIRY
AND A GOAT WHO BE CALLED MARY
WHO GIVES US
WHAT WE
NEEEEEEED.

OUR BODIES MAY BE STINKING
OUR BRAINS MAY NOT BE THINKING
BUT BY THE FIRE WE BE DRINKING
TROLL ALE IN GOBLETS CLINKING
AS THE WORLD BE A SHRINKING
AND OUR EYES KEEP ON BLINKING
AT THE SUN THAT IS SINKING
IN THE SKYYYYYYYY

'That is a really bad song,' whispered Bridget the Brave, from behind the rock where she and Miika were hiding. 'It's the worst song I've ever heard. And I once happened to witness the Elfhelm *Daily Snow* Music and Spickle Dancing Festival, so that's really saying something.'

'It's terrible,' agreed Miika, peeping out from behind the rock. 'My ears want to fall off. But they must be singing it for a reason. It seems to be some kind of ceremony. Look, one of the trolls is getting up. That troll with only one eye . . .'

And it was true. As the troll song continued, a one-eyed troll slowly stood up and headed into a dark cave where she disappeared.

'Maybe she's gone to get something,' whispered Miika.

'I wonder what it could be,' said Bridget the Brave, but the next verse of the troll song offered some clues.

TONIGHT THERE BE A BREEZE
THAT MAKE OUR TROLL TOES FREEZE
IT BE COMING THROUGH THE TREES
BUT WE SIT HERE ON OUR KNEES
OUR LUMPY HANDS WILL SEIZE
THE THING THAT MAKES US PLEASED
(ALL TROUBLES WILL BE EASED!)
WITH THIS URGA-BURGA CHEESE
IT'S SO GOOOOOOOOOOOOOOOD

'Oh wow,' muttered Bridget the Brave. 'I've heard about this! It's the Troll Cheese Ceremony. It's one of the most important events in the whole troll calendar.'

'That,' said Miika, 'is *not* a good thing.'

With heavy, thumping footsteps that echoed around the valley, the giant one-eyed troll returned from the cave, holding a huge jar of something that Miika couldn't quite see in the fading light. But, to be honest, he didn't need to see it. He could *smell* it. The smell was so strong and pungent it reached the two tiny mouse noses hidden far up the craggy slope.

'Oh wow,' said Miika. 'Oh my goodness me! That *smell*. It's beautiful. It's heavenly. It's like nothing else I have ever smelled before in my entire life.'

'I told you,' said Bridget the Brave knowingly. 'But, trust me, just wait till it's right under your nose. Just wait till it's in your mouth!'

The Flying Cheese

Miika closed his eyes and focused on breathing in the smell. For a moment he forgot he was sitting on the slope of the most dangerous valley in the entire world. He opened his eyes to see the giant troll pulling the cheese out of the jar and holding it up to the sky. And then the trolls all stopped singing and began chanting loudly instead.

Urga-Burga!

Urga-Burga!

Urga-Burga!

Miika twitched his whiskers. He was scared.

'I didn't think it would be like this,' he said. 'I thought the cheese would be on its own somewhere. I didn't think we'd have to steal the cheese right from under their noses.'

Bridget the Brave was shaking her head. 'No, no. This is perfect. They've shown us exactly where the cheese is. They've brought it out to us. And that means we don't have to go any further into the valley. We can stay right here where they can't see us and we don't have to go down there and get stamped on by any giant feet. Not with you and your magic drimwicky powers, my friend. You just have to wish for it and make the cheese move through the air.'

'But they'll see it!' wailed Miika, staring back at the forest, ready to run home and forget the whole idea. 'They'll see the cheese flying through the air towards us!'

'Miika, Miika, Miika, Miika . . . I've thought it all through. The cheese will fly into the heart of the Wooded Hills, straight to the Hollow Tree. The trolls won't find it. No one ever goes to that part of the forest. No pixies, no elves, no trolls, no one! It'll be ours for ever. Look at the size of it! That'll keep both of us going for an entire lifetime.'

'But it'll be impossible to get away with this.'

Bridget the Brave shook her head. 'Impossibility is just a possibility you don't understand yet. Remember? Nothing is impossible. Not now you're drimwicked. And trolls are stupid. They're even more stupid than elves. They're *even* more stupid than humans. And that's saying something. They are really, really, really, really, *really* stupid. And anyway, they can't see very well, so it'll be fine. Even if they were looking in this direction they wouldn't see us up here.' She turned away from Miika and looked back towards the fire and the trolls and the noise of sudden excitement down in the valley. 'But, Miika, you have to be quick! They're about to eat it!'

And Miika saw that it was true. The one-eyed troll, illuminated by the orange glow of the fire, was getting ready to break up the cheese.

'Now, let's be eating the Urga-burga,' she said, in a booming voice as rough and hard as the rocks all around the valley.

'YES, LUMPELLA!' shouted the trolls with great noise and enthusiasm. 'LET'S BE EATING THE URGA-BURGA!'

'Now,' whispered Bridget the Brave in Miika's ear. 'Do it now before she divides the cheese. Now! *Now!*'

Miika was already doing it. He had closed his eyes and was focusing on the smell of that most incredible cheese as it trembled in Lumpella's giant hands.

'WHAT BE HAPPENING, LUMPELLA?' asked one of the trolls, as the giant piece of Urga-burga cheese shone with magical blue light.

'SOMETHING BAD BE HAPPENING!' said another troll, who

also only had one eye. (Most of the other trolls had two eyes. Apart from the one with three.)

'I CAN SEE IT BE BAD, THUD,' said Lumpella, as the cheese rose out of her hands towards the sky.

And the trolls all stood up and tried to grab it. Thud managed to reach it and hold on for a second before the large chunk of cheese shot out of his hands and flew through the sky like a giant blue meteor, over Miika and Bridget the Brave's heads and fast over the distant pine and birch trees.

Miika saw, in his mind, the cheese travelling over the dark forest, and the Truth Pixie's cottage, then turning sharply east as soon as it reached Elfhelm. He saw it flying over the Street of Seven Curves and Reindeer Field and Vodol Street, over the Tower and the *Daily Snow* headquarters, through the trees, past Bridget the Brave's home and beyond the fallen branch, all the way to the Hollow Tree. Then, in his mind, he let go and opened his eyes.

He was exhausted.

'You did it!' squealed Bridget the Brave.

'I, um, yes, I, um, wow, I think so,' said Miika, bewildered and breathless. 'I really think I did.'

'Let's go and look!'

So, they scurried up the craggy slope and back into the forest, as the trolls ran about in all directions, bumping into each other and staring frantically up at the sky. '**THIS BE BIG, BIG BAD**,' one said, before accidentally stepping on the fire. '**OW!**'

The ground thundered with the force of the trolls' footsteps. Rocks and stones fell all around Miika and Bridget the Brave, and dust rose in clouds, making them cough and splutter as they scrabbled back up the valley. Eventually the air cleared and they were free, scampering back through the forest towards the Hollow Tree, in search of the best cheese in the universe.

The Best Taste in the Universe

'I've never tasted anything like it,' said Miika. He and Bridget the Brave were back in the tree hole, staring at the large chunk of Urgaburga they had broken off from the even larger chunk that was sitting in the Hollow Tree, seven trees along. He took another nibble. 'It is so creamy but also firm. So tangy yet sweet. So nutty yet also fruity. Smoky but *piquant* too. Strong and yet also delicate. Light *and* pleasantly heavy. It's a cheese made of opposites – like tasting everything good in the world *all at once.*'

Bridget the Brave nodded an I-told-you-so nod. 'Exactly. It is more than cheese. It is *life*. You can say what you like about trolls. And they do have their faults – like rampant destruction and murder and world record-breaking levels of stupidity – but they do know how to make really good cheese.'

'But they'll find it eventually. They'll smell it out. They'll find the Hollow Tree.'

Miika remembered the fear he had felt when his mum had shouted to all her baby mice about the stolen mushroom.

Bridget the Brave shook her head. 'Trolls actually have a very bad sense of smell. Well, that's what I've heard. They have these giant ugly noses which are utterly useless at smelling.' But Bridget the Brave didn't seem entirely convinced by her own words. 'Besides, they hate leaving Troll Valley. And even if they did, they would never suspect two little forest mice, now, would they?'

'Oh, I don't know,' said Miika. 'I just have a phenomenally bad feeling that stealing a mountain of cheese from trolls is going to have . . . consequences.'

Bridget the Brave considered. 'Which is why we should keep on eating the evidence.

Morning, noon and night. And the great thing is . . . it will never run out.'

Miika ate some more. 'It really is delicious. But if it will never run out, how will we eat the evidence?'

Bridget the Brave flapped her tiny arms in frustration. 'You and your questions, Miika! Questions, questions – they're fine, of course, but they don't taste very good. Unlike Urga-burga.'

He thought about what his sister Yala had said just before he left his family. *If you find enough cheese to live on, you will never – and I repeat NEVER – want for anything else. That is as good as life gets.*'

And maybe this was it. Maybe this really was as good as life got. Maybe he should stop worrying. Maybe he should just hang out with his friend and eat scrumptious cheese for ever. But something wasn't right. He had a feeling that he couldn't quite understand. A kind of sense, maybe because of his drimwick powers, that trouble was coming.

As he took another bite of delectable cheese, he really tried to believe that everything was going to be okay.

How the Stars Shine

The next morning, in the fireside warmth of the Truth Pixie's cottage, Miika tried to ask the pixie a question without giving too much away.

The Truth Pixie was busy painting a picture. It was just an entirely white canvas which she was covering in white paint. 'I am calling this one *The Inside of an Elf's Head*. It's very minimal.'

'It's, um, beautiful,' Miika said. 'Yes, very minimal . . .'

'Liar.'

Miika finally got to the point. 'Do you think everything is going to be okay?'

The Truth Pixie paused, her paintbrush in mid-air. 'What kind of question is that?'

'A worried one.'

'What is it that you're worried about?'

'I . . . I can't tell you. But I just need to know. About the future.'

She pointed the paintbrush in the mouse's direction. 'Miika, I am a *truth pixie*. Not a *fortune-telling pixie*. I know a lot of things, of course, and I'm very smart. But I don't know all the things that haven't happened yet.'

Miika sighed, his tail drooping like a string that had lost its balloon. 'I just need some words of reassurance.'

'Well, I can reassure you that terrible things will probably happen.'

'Great.'

'Terrible things *always* happen.'

'Thanks.'

'But good things will also happen. Because that is what life is. You need the bad to know what good is. You need the dark to know the light.'

Miika thought of how Urga–burga cheese tasted. All the opposites mixed together, complementing each other like in life itself.

'I mean,' continued the Truth Pixie, 'think of a night sky. The stars wouldn't shine without all the darkness around them, would they?'

Miika twitched his whiskers.

'So, bad things and good things will happen. But the good things will feel even better because of the bad things having happened. And sometimes good things grow out of the bad things.'

'Right,' he said, his tail curling up into the shape of a question mark. 'Thank you. I think I feel a bit happier now.'

'But happiness,' said the Truth Pixie, standing back to get a better look at her painting, 'has nothing to do with good things or bad things.'

'It doesn't?'

'No. I once knew a pixie over in the Eastern Lakes who was the unluckiest pixie you could imagine. She was *so* unlucky. Once she fell down a well and her wings broke off and she was stuck down there for a whole week. But, you know, she spent the whole time singing the old pixie classic "I'm a Happy Pixie, A Really Happy Pixie (Oh, Yes I Am)" with a big smile on her face. Right there, at the bottom of a well! And that's how they found her, because they could hear her happy song from across the fields.' The Truth Pixie sighed. 'So it just shows you, my little mouse acquaintance, that it's not *what* happens to you in life. It's how you choose to *deal with what happens.* And you're not like me. You haven't been cursed to be one thing for ever. You can change at any moment. You can switch from truth to lies and lies to truth. You can switch from worry to calm. From timid to brave. From selfish to kind. You don't have to be what other people think you are. And really, if you think about—'

But she didn't utter another word. In fact, she couldn't. Because just at that moment she was knocked right off her feet.

BOOM!

And just at that same moment Miika was sent flying into the air. And the Truth Pixie's pot of white paint splattered all over the floorboards.

'Now, that was not normal,' said the Truth Pixie, picking herself up and rushing over to the window to see what had caused the gigantic thud. 'Well, this *is* interesting . . .'

Miika's heart raced as he lay flat on his back. 'What's interesting?'

But then he lifted his head just enough to be able to see across the room to the window. To see, beyond the garden, the end of a giant, grey, dusty, hairy troll leg sticking out from below a shawl of goatskins and an equally giant, grey, dusty, hairy troll foot landing with another—

BOOM!

'It's a troll!' said the Truth Pixie. 'And it's heading for Elfhelm!'

Miika felt fear flood through his whole body. 'Oh no,' he said. '*Oh no.*'

Miika's Panic

hy would a troll be heading for Elfhelm?' said the Truth Pixie.

The question swirled like a cyclone in Miika's mind.

Why WOULD a troll be heading for Elfhelm? Why WOULD a TROLL be heading for Elfhelm? Why WOULD a TROLL be heading for ELFHELM? WHY WOULD . . .

'Oh no,' said Miika, jumping to his feet. 'Oh no. Oh no. OH NO.'

The Truth Pixie was confused. 'Miika? What's the matter? I mean, apart from the giant troll? Why have you got a guilty look on your face?'

'I've, um, got to go,' he squeaked.

And Miika ran. He squeezed himself under the yellow door and kept running as he headed down the path that wound through the trees, all the way to Elfhelm, following the giant footprints in the snow.

A Cheese Thief

The troll was standing in the middle of Reindeer Field. All the reindeer and about a hundred elves were looking up at him. It was one of the trolls Miika had seen by the fire. One of those with only a single eye. Thud. That was his name.

Miika darted through the crowd of elves to see what was going on, and just then the troll began to speak in his booming voice.

'I BE HERE WITH A WARN-ING!' he said.

Father Topo stepped out of the crowd. 'We don't want any trouble.'

'WELL, TROUBLE BE WHAT YOU BE GETTING, YOU EVIL LITTLE BUMFLIES!'

'I can assure you,' said Mother Harkus, covering one of her school pupil's pointed ears, 'that we are not evil and we are not bumflies and we've done nothing to upset you. We are just living happy, peaceful lives.'

'HAHAHAHAHAHAHA HAHA! BE TELLING THAT TO THE TROLL WHOSE HEAD EXPLODED IN THE TOWER!'

'Ah,' said Father Topo. 'I know the incident you're talking about. But that was over a year ago now. And Elfhelm was a very different place back then. We had a tough leader.'

'VODOL.'

'That's right. But now things have changed. We don't lock people up in the Tower any more. And, as Mother Harkus just said, we are just trying to live peaceful lives. Plus, technically, it wasn't an elf who made that particular troll's head explode.'

Miika said nothing. He wondered if

Father Topo was going to tell the troll that it was, in fact, the Truth Pixie who had done that, when she had been locked in the Tower with Nikolas. But Father Topo wasn't the type to land anyone in trouble, not even the Truth Pixie.

'So,' said Father Topo, 'we are all very sorry about any trouble that has happened in the past. Just as I am sure you trolls are sorry about all the rampaging you have done over the years. But these are better times. These are happier times. Let's put all that behind us. Let's not worry about things that happened years ago, shall we?'

This made Thud very angry. His bearded face turned a bit red and he smashed his big brown teeth together. 'YEARS??? IT BE YESTERDAY!!!'

Miika gulped, and hid behind the feet of Mother Mocha, from the Bank of Chocolate.

'What are you talking about?' asked Father Topo.

And then it came. The word Miika had

been dreading. And in the loudest voice Miika had ever heard.

'CHEEEEEEEEEEEEEEE-EEEEEEEEEESE!'

Noosh turned to her great-great-great-great-great-grandfather. 'Did he just say cheese?'

'Yes,' said Father Topo. 'I believe he did.'

'WHO STOLE THE URGA-BURGA?' roared Thud.

'What's Urga-burga?' asked Noosh.

'I believe it is a variety of cheese,' said Father Topo. 'Listen,' he said, addressing the troll. 'I think you've made a mistake. No one has stolen anything from you. Elves don't steal.'

'And certainly not cheese,' said Moodon the elf. 'My wife makes very tasty cheese and she shares it with everyone.'

'Thanks, darling,' Loka told her husband, squeezing his hand. 'That's very kind of you.'

But Thud wasn't having any of it.

'ONE OF YOU HERE BE

A THIEF! IF THEY WHO BE A THIEF DOES NOT BE SAYING THEY BE A THIEF THEN THERE BE TROUBLE. IF NO ONE OWNS UP, THERE BE A HUNDRED TROLLS HERE BY DARKNESS AND WE BE SMASHING EVERYTHING!'

Miika's little body started to shake like a birch leaf in the breeze. This was all his fault.

Then another person stepped forward. And this person spoke in a voice that Miika recognised instantly. It was the voice he knew better than any voice in the entire world.

It was Nikolas. The human boy. He was walking across the snow, passing Blitzen and Dancer, to get closer to Thud.

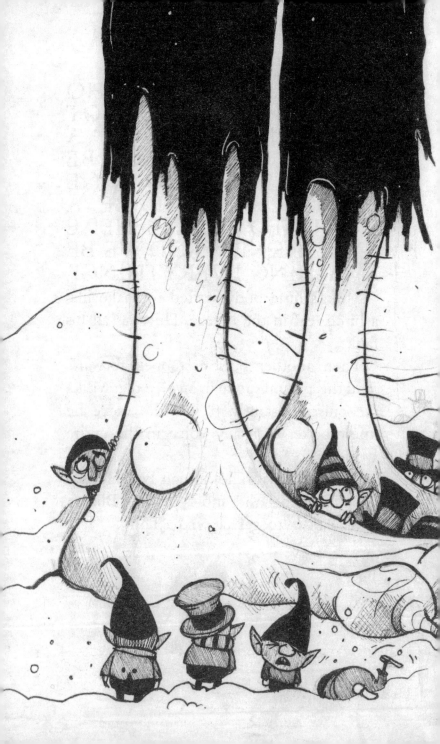

The troll bent over and scratched his head. He had clearly never seen a human before.

'Please, Mr Troll. Elves don't steal things. It's against their nature.'

Thud frowned, and then shouted so loud he nearly knocked Nikolas off his feet. 'YOU BE NOT ELF! MAYBE YOU BE URGA-BURGA THIEF!'

Nikolas stayed quiet for a long time.

Miika wondered what was going through his mind.

Nikolas was clever. And kind. And if there was anyone who could calm an angry troll down, it was probably him.

And then, finally, Nikolas said it. 'It was me.'

'WHAT BE YOU?'

'It was me who stole the cheese,' Nikolas lied.

Gasps and murmurs filled the air. Miika noticed Blitzen was looking angrily up at the giant troll, pawing his front hoof in the snow, as if preparing to charge.

And just then Thud's hand swooped down and scooped Nikolas high into the air.

'TAKE ME TO THE CHEESE!' he roared.

'I can't do that, actually,' said Nikolas, from inside the troll's fist.

'THEN I BE TAKING YOU!'

And with that, Blitzen galloped at the troll. He flew into the air and aimed towards Thud's one eye, antlers angled forward. But Thud saw the reindeer just in time and batted him away with the hand that wasn't holding tight to Nikolas, as if Blitzen was just a fly. A fly sent soaring and spinning towards the Tower, which Blitzen managed to swerve just in time.

Miika had never felt so terrible in all his

life. This was worse than falling off a reindeer's antlers to certain death. This was worse than saying goodbye to his entire family. This was even worse than the time when the Truth Pixie had been sick on him after making herself dizzy.

I am a thief, thought Miika. *And I have always been a thief. Ever since I stole that mushroom from my mum.*

He knew he wouldn't be able to help Nikolas or the elves. He knew he would stay silent. He just had to face it. He was who he had always been.

A selfish mouse. A thief. And a coward.

Big Things and Small Things

The troll had started to walk away, back in the direction of Troll Valley, with Nikolas still in his fist, when he turned to ask the population of Elfhelm one last question.

'WHO BE KNOWING WHERE THE URGA-BURGA IS?'

And there was silence. The kind of silence Miika had known before. A silence that felt a bit wobbly and weird, and made his tummy feel weak.

A hundred elves looked at one another. They shrugged their shoulders.

The silence kept on being silence.

But then Miika heard a voice.

'Me,' the voice said.

He realised it was his own voice.

And he was saying it again, a little louder. He was telling the truth – without the Truth Pixie even being there. He remembered what the Truth Pixie had said about changing, about how he could switch from truth to lies and from lies to truth, from timid to brave, from selfish to kind. *You don't have to be what other people think you are.*

Miika realised at that very moment that it wasn't what other people thought of him that was the problem. The problem was what he thought of himself.

Ever since he had stolen the mushroom from his family he had believed deep down that he was a thief and a coward. But he didn't have to be any of those things.

He looked around at all the elves. At Nikolas. At the Truth Pixie, who had just arrived and was coming through the crowd. He saw Loka, and her sparkling eyes, who had so often given him tasty cheese out of pure kindness. He knew that he didn't want any trouble to come to any of them. Ever. They were his friends. He loved them all.

And that was all you needed to be brave. Love. His older sister had been wrong all that time ago. You couldn't live life just looking after yourself. You had to live with yourself too. And he wanted to live not as who he had become. But as who he could be.

So he said it again. But this time louder. 'ME!'

And now *all* the elves were looking at him, as he walked over the crisp, snow-sprinkled ground towards the troll, and he felt something he had never really felt before. Something he didn't even know he had inside him.

Something called courage.

Thud looked around, confused. His forehead was creased like a bedsheet after a bad dream. 'WHO SAID THAT?'

Miika gulped. He was petrified. His blood turned to ice. But still he kept walking until he was right in front of Thud.

Courage, he realised, wasn't about not feeling scared. It was about feeling scared and keeping going anyway, standing in front of someone a thousand times your size, and trying to help a friend out of trouble.

'Me. Look. Down here. The mouse. That's me.'

And then Thud – still squeezing Nikolas in his hand – saw the small brown animal in the snow, no larger than a leaf.

'YOU BE A MOUSE,' said Thud, his one eye looking down at Miika.

'Yes,' said Miika. 'I be a mouse. I mean . . . I am a mouse.'

Nikolas shouted up at the troll. 'Don't hurt him! He's just a little mouse. He doesn't know what he's saying. Do you, Miika? I mean, look at the size of him. How could he steal a big lump of anything?'

The troll laughed and agreed. Trolls, generally, have a deep disrespect for all small creatures. The whole world, according to troll philosophy, is divided into two types of things. Big things and small things. Big things are good and strong, and small things are bad and weak, and Miika was definitely – in Thud's eye – too weak to have stolen a huge piece of Urga-burga.

'NO! BE NOT A MOUSE! A MOUSE BE NOT MAGIC! URGA-BURGA FLY! A MOUSE NOT BE MAKING URGA-BURGA FLY! WHO BE YOU STEALING IT WITH?'

'No one. No one at all. It was just me. It was all my idea.'

'HAHAHAHAHAHAHAHA-HAHAHAHAHAHAHAHA!' laughed Thud.

Miika closed his eyes and wished.

He wished very hard to save his human friend and all the elves. He took his mind over to the east, to the Wooded Hills, through the trees and their snow-heavy branches, on and on to the dark inner space of the Hollow Tree. He saw the cheese and wished it to rise, and then he wished it high into the sky, higher than the tallest tree. And then he wished it to fly to the Street of Seven Curves and over all the houses and shops and halls of Elfhelm.

He wished that special stinky cheese over the frozen lake and Reindeer Field until it was right in front of the troll's face. The elves gasped in surprise.

'Well, that was unexpected!' said Noosh.

'THE URGA-BURGA!' exclaimed Thud, his eye wide in surprise. 'THE URGA-BURGA BE FLYING!'

His face went from shock to a smile and then to a laugh of delight as he stamped his feet in earth-shaking glee, causing most of the elves to lose their balance and topple over. 'URGA-BURGA! URGA-BURGA!'

Thud's hand opened and Nikolas fell through the air. He landed safely on the back of Blitzen as the trusty reindeer dived through the air to meet him.

The troll seemed so happy, as he took the giant boulder of hovering blue cheese in his hands, that Nikolas began to laugh along nervously. And Father Topo and Noosh laughed too. And then Mother Harkus laughed. And then Loka and Moodon laughed. And then all the elves laughed. And then, even Miika laughed.

But he soon stopped laughing when a shadow crept over him and he saw one of Thud's bare feet – his right – had lifted very slowly off the ground and was directly above his head. Miika looked up and could see the hairs of his large toes dangling over like a spider's legs.

And all the laughter suddenly stopped.

Thud stamped his foot down on Miika so hard it shook the whole country and caused the King of Finland, hundreds of miles away in his castle, to spill his morning cup of cloudberry juice.

Flattened

Miika was squashed flat. Right there on the ground. Flatter than a trodden leaf. Flatter than pastry. Flatter than a bookmark. Flatter than this page you're reading right now.

Thud leaned over to inspect his stamping, his one eye squinting shrewdly.

'GOOD! MOUSE BE DEAD! LET THAT BE WARNING TO THIEFS WHO STEAL CHEEEEEEEEEEEEEESE!'

And then, satisfied, he walked away with giant stomping footsteps, carrying the vast lump of cheese all the way back to Troll Valley.

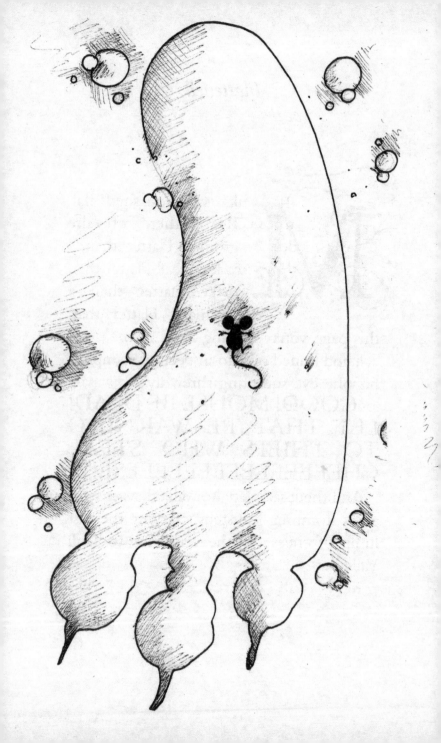

Things That Are Even More Important Than Cheese

But, of course, Miika wasn't really dead.

He couldn't die.

He'd been drimwicked.

But even though he'd been drimwicked, he could still be squashed flat. His body started to transform, bulging from a flat-as-a-bookmark to a normal-round-mouse shape.

'Aaagh,' he said, as he opened his eyes to see Nikolas and Noosh and Blitzen and the Truth Pixie above him. 'Eeek.'

But alongside the weird sensation of a body popping back into shape he felt something else.

He felt a fullness that wasn't just to do with his body.

He felt, possibly for the first time ever, entirely himself.

A complete Miika.

Blitzen gave him a lick, pleased to find him still alive. The lick was disgusting.

'It's okay, Miika,' said Noosh. 'You're still alive. And that nasty, stinky troll has stomped off back to the valley.'

'And he's taken the cheese with him,' said Nikolas, crouching down beside his mouse friend.

Miika sighed. 'I'm sorry about all this. I didn't mean to steal the cheese.' He saw the Truth Pixie's doubting eyes. 'Well, I did actually. I did mean to steal it. And it was really tasty cheese. And there was enough to live on for ever. But I realised that some things are more important than cheese . . . even excellent cheese.'

Nikolas smiled. It was the same smile he'd given the mouse the first day they'd met, after he had saved Miika from his father's axe. 'You're a brave mouse, Miika. Kind and courageous. I've always seen it, even if you haven't. And the thing with courage is that you sometimes don't know it's in you until you really need it.'

And these words felt good. Maybe even as good as the taste of troll cheese.

Just then Miika realised there was something he had to do.

Something that filled him with almost as much dread as a troll's huge, hairy stomping foot.

'Um, I've really got to go,' he told Nikolas and the elves. 'See you later.'

And he scrambled to his feet and headed out into the snow, trying to find one little bit of extra bravery, because he knew he was going to need it where he was going.

As Close to Shouting as a Mouse Can Get

Bridget the Brave was stomping around in her tree hole, kicking birch leaves. She was clearly not happy.

In fact, to say Bridget the Brave was not happy was like saying a cat was not a bicycle.

She was really, really, *really* not happy.

Just listen . . .

'I am not happy,' she said, twitching her tail in frustration.

'I know,' said Miika, cowering in the corner of the tree hole.

'Don't you see what you've done? You've given away a lifetime's supply of cheese. And not just any old cheese. The most dreamy and delicious cheese in the entire universe! And you did it without asking me. The absolute cheek of it!'

'I couldn't ask you,' said Miika, nervously stroking his whiskers. 'There was no time. No time at all. Thud was threatening to destroy Elfhelm. He was threatening to kill the elves. He was going to kidnap Nikolas.'

'So?'

'So? Nikolas is my friend! And so are the elves!'

Bridget the Brave huffed. 'Am *I* not your friend?'

'I don't know, to be honest,' squeaked Miika.

'*What?!*' Bridget the Brave stopped stomping and turned to look straight at Miika.

'Well, I saved your life and all you did was insult me for it. And you only seem to like me if I can give you something. You only made friends with me again so I could steal the cheese from the trolls. And it *is* stealing. Not taking.'

At that, Bridget the Brave got very angry

indeed and started to shout. Well, as close to shouting as a mouse can get, which isn't particularly close.

'You are a stupid, *stupid* mouse.' She shook her head. 'No. Not even that. You are a stupid, stupid *nothing*. You will never be a mouse. You are not like any other mouse in the whole world. You are a pathetic little creature. You are worse than a troll because at least a troll is a troll. You are not one thing or another. You are a pathetic *in-between* kind of creature. Not true mammal, not true magic—'

'Bridget the Brave, please stop,' Miika squeaked.

But Bridget the Brave wasn't going to stop. 'You had one chance. One chance of *being something*. One chance of adventure. No one would have ever found the Hollow Tree. No one would have ever known. We could have been thieves and legends and *full of cheese for ever*. You gave away our happiness for a life of dull, old mushrooms.'

'But we *can* have cheese! I know an elf called Loka who—'

Bridget the Brave mimicked Miika cruelly. '*I know an elf called Loka who* . . . Have you heard yourself? What freaky kind of a mouse likes elves and pixies?'

Miika thought about this for a little while. Once upon a time, Bridget the Brave's words would have upset him. But now he realised that it really was a choice. Bridget the Brave's opinion of Miika didn't have to be Miika's opinion of Miika.

'Tell me!' Bridget the Brave went on. 'What . . . kind . . . of . . . mouse?'

'A *me* kind of mouse,' Miika said. 'That is the kind of mouse I am. And I don't need you to like me any more, Bridget the Brave. You can think whatever you want. And to be honest, I didn't like the feeling of being a thief. Even a cheese thief. Yes, Urga–burga is delicious. But no cheese tastes as good as being kind feels. And that's what I want to be. I want to be a kind creature. And sometimes the very bravest thing is to be who you want to be.'

'Ugh!' grumbled Bridget the Brave. 'You sound just like an elf!'

'Well, I'm not an elf. But, as I said, you can think what you like about me. So, see you around.'

And with that, Miika left Bridget the Brave's tree hole and went out into the cold, clear air and started to walk home.

'Hey!' shouted Bridget the Brave after him. 'Hey! Come back, you stupid non-mouse! Hey! Miika! Miika! Stop ignoring me! Hey! Hey!'

But Miika kept going. He scurried over the snow, weaving past rocks and pine cones, and he didn't look back once.

It's How Things End That Matters

That evening, Nikolas, Father Topo and Noosh came to visit Miika in the Truth Pixie's cottage.

Father Topo wanted to show Miika the latest front page of the *Daily Snow*. The Truth Pixie was warming a sweet bumbleberry pie in the oven.

'Look at that headline,' he said excitedly. 'MOUSE VERSUS TROLL: THE CASE OF THE MISSING CHEESE! Look, Miika, look there in the second paragraph. They call you a hero. *And then our mouse hero used his new magic powers* . . .'

'I was hardly a hero. I nearly caused Elfhelm to be destroyed and Nikolas to be kidnapped. I was a cheese thief.'

'Well, yes,' said Nikolas, who was sitting cross-legged on the floor, with his red hat in his hands and his head touching the ceiling. 'That's true. You *were* a cheese thief. But you did the right thing in the end. And it's how things end that matters.' Nikolas had tears in his eyes. 'And there's nothing more important in the whole world than a good friend.'

'Well, that's kind of you to say,' Miika said, smoothing his tummy fur. 'You're a good friend too.'

And Nikolas lowered his head and frowned and gave Miika a slightly guilty look. 'And I'm sorry I haven't had much time for you recently. I'm going to be a better friend to you. I've been spending far too much time at Elf Council meetings. And not enough time with you.'

'Thank you, Nikolas. I love you, dear friend – with all my heart.'

The Truth Pixie looked like she was going to be sick. 'Oh, please. No soppiness here. This is a pixie house. It's forbidden.'

'Well, you're a good friend too, Truth Pixie,' said Miika. 'Like it or not.'

The Truth Pixie crinkled her face in disgust. 'Gross.'

Miika smiled, looking at the snow falling outside the window.

Meanwhile, Noosh leaned back in the rocking chair, with a spinning top resting on her lap. 'I've been wondering, Miika . . . Did anyone make you do it?'

Miika shook his head. He may no longer be friends with Bridget the Brave but he didn't want to get anyone into trouble. 'No,' he said softly. 'No one.'

'He's lying,' said the Truth Pixie, who could spot a lie from a mile away. She put her hand over her mouth. 'Sorry. I shouldn't have said that. But you know me, I just can't help it.'

Miika sighed. 'Well, there might have been someone else involved. But I didn't have to steal the cheese. It was up to me. And I used my powers badly.'

'Well,' said Father Topo, smiling, 'I did warn Noosh it was dangerous to drimwick a mouse!'

Miika smiled.

'Magic is a gift. It's precious. You have to handle it with care,' said Father Topo.

Miika nodded a tiny mouse nod. 'I will, I promise. There's more to life than cheese. I know that now.'

Then Nikolas remembered something and pulled a little parcel out of his pocket. 'Oh! Talking of cheese, Loka asked me to give you this. It might not be a lifetime's supply but it should at least get you to the end of the year. It's a new variety of cheese. She's calling it . . . Miika's Delight.'

Nikolas placed the parcel in front of Miika and unwrapped it for him. It was a pale cheese with what looked like bits of nut in it. Noosh broke off a morsel for Miika, who sniffed it and nibbled it. It had a very delicate taste. A taste that took a while to truly notice and understand, but which was really rather lovely.

It wasn't Urga-burga cheese, but in a way it was even better. Because this cheese had been made with love and given to him by someone who cared.

'Miika's Delight,' said the mouse. 'That's catchy. I may be biased, but I think it's a very good name. I think it will be a best-seller.'

And Miika thought he would save a bit. And tomorrow he would take it into the Wooded Hills and leave a little bit outside Bridget the Brave's tree hole. Even if they weren't friends any more, he still wanted her to taste good things.

Just then, a little bell rang to indicate that the pie was ready. And Miika soon discovered that cheese went surprisingly well with warm, sugary bumbleberry pie.

'Mmmm,' said Father Topo, thanking the Truth Pixie. 'This is delicious. We should have this again at Christmas.'

Noosh became suddenly excited. 'Oooh, Christmas! It's so exciting! Only one hundred and eighty-eight sleeps to go!'

A Happy Mouse

After Nikolas and the elves had gone home, Miika curled up on the warm fireside rug.

'Well, that was quite a day, wasn't it, Truth Pixie?'

The pixie was tucked up in her little bed. 'It was. Quite a day. And quite a pie.'

Miika sighed with agreement. His eyes felt heavy as he looked into the fire, watching the glow of the embers gently fade away.

'I think I used to worry too much about fitting in.'

'Yes. Same here. It's quite rare I agree with you, or anyone in fact, but the truth is, not everyone will like us. Not everyone we meet will always want the best for us. And not everyone will know our truth. If people want to hate us, it's easier to let them. You see, it is better to be disliked for being who you are than to be liked for who you are not. Being who you are not is exhausting.'

Miika yawned and nodded.

'Be you,' the Truth Pixie continued. 'Be the full you. Don't try to make yourself small to match someone else. And, sure, fitting in is fine. But it's not as great as standing out. Standing out is' – she searched for the word – '*outstanding*.'

Miika smiled softly. 'Thank you, Truth Pixie.'

'Hey, don't thank me. Thank the truth.'

'Thanks, truth.'

And they were quiet for a little while.

'Miika?' said the Truth Pixie sleepily.

'Yes?' said Miika.

'I'm glad you're here.'

'Thank you, Truth Pixie. I'm glad I'm here too. And I'm glad you're here. I'm glad *we're* here.'

And with that, the mouse rested his eyes, ready for sleep.

He felt, for once, grateful to be who he was.

In a way, Bridget the Brave had been right. He wasn't one thing or another thing. But why would he want to be? He wasn't half this or half that. He was a whole *himself.*

Yes, he thought to himself, *there is no one else I would rather be than me.*

A warm mouse.

A sleepy mouse.

A happy mouse.

A mouse called Miika.

Acknowledgements

A massive thank you to you for reading this book. I thought you read it very well and smiled in most of the right places.

And of course to the brilliant genius of illustration Chris Mould, who somehow manages to take a scene from my brain and put it into wonderful life. Also a big thank you to my agent Clare Conville and all the elves at C&W. Thanks also go to my editor Francis Bickmore, who has been editing my books for longer than a pine tree grows in Elfhelm. And to Rafi Romaya for her wonderful art direction. And to the whole of Canongate Books, every pixie's favourite publisher in the Far North. In particular to Megan Reid, Vicki Rutherford, Leila Cruickshank, Lucy Zhou, Alice Shortland, Jenny Fry, Jess Neale, Caro Clarke, Jo Lord, Steph Scott, Kate Oliver, Caroline

Gorham, Laura Wilkie, Kate Gibb and not forgetting Jamie Byng.

And lastly to the wonderful humans I live with, to Andrea my first reader and the friend I can always be myself with, and my children Lucas and Pearl who always tell me when we need more Blitzen or Truth Pixie.

Turn the page to read the first chapter of
A Boy Called Christmas, now a major film!

'The most evergreen, immortal Christmas
story for decades'
Stephen Fry

CANON▌▌GATE

An Ordinary Boy

You are about to read the true story of Father Christmas.

Yes. Father Christmas.

You may wonder how I know the true story of Father Christmas, and I will tell you that you shouldn't really question such things. Not right at the start of a book. It's rude, for one thing. All you need to understand is that I do know the story of Father Christmas, or else why would I be writing it?

Maybe you don't call him Father Christmas.

Maybe you call him something else.

Santa or Saint Nick or Santa Claus or Sinterklaas or Kris Kringle or Pelznickel or Papa Noël or Strange Man With A Big Belly Who Talks To Reindeer And Gives Me Presents. Or maybe you have a name you've come up with yourself, just for fun. If you were an elf, though, you would always call him Father Christmas. It was the pixies who started calling him Santa Claus, and spread the word, just to confuse things, in their mischievous way.

But whatever you happen to call him, you know about him, and that's the main thing.

Can you believe there was a time when no one knew about him? A time when he was just an ordinary boy called Nikolas, living in the middle of nowhere, or the middle of Finland, doing nothing with magic except believing in it? A boy who knew very little about the world except the taste of mushroom soup, the feel of a cold north wind, and the stories he was told. And who only had a doll made out of a turnip to play with.

But life was going to change for Nikolas, in ways he could never have imagined. Things were going to happen to him.

Good things.

Bad things.

Impossible things.

But if you are one of those people who believe that some things are impossible, you should put this book down right away. It is most certainly not for you.

Because this book is full of *impossible things*.

'A glorious mix of fairytale, folklore and fun'
Francesca Simon

CANON||GATE

'The perfect package of happiness'
Olivia Colman

CANON‖GATE

ACTIVITIES FOR YOU

The fun's not over yet! There are three exciting activities in store for you, starting with a little exercise to test your knowledge below.

Read the passage and answer the questions below:

Two mice were sitting in a forest, leaning against a pine cone.

They were friends. And they looked quite ordinary. They had ordinary dark eyes, ordinary pink noses, ordinary tails.

Where they lived, though, was quite *un*-ordinary. Because where they lived was the Far North.

At the very top of a country that humans call Finland is a little town called Elfhelm, which is the most unique place on the whole planet. A place you won't find on any map. A place full of brightly coloured wooden houses in winding streets. A place full of elves, and flying reindeer, and the occasional pixie.

Q1. How are the mice described in the extract?
Underline key words.
Q2. Where would you find Finland on a map?
What about Elfhelm?
Q3. How is Elfhelm presented as a special place?
What magic might you find there?

SAY CHEESE!

Draw your very own world-famous cheese to be desired
by all the mice across the land.

Don't forget to give it a memorable name and list the
secret ingredients that make it so delicious!

Name of cheese:	
Description:	Secret Ingredients:
Drawing:	

MICE TO MEET YOU

Read the description of Miika from page 3:

'He was the less scruffy of the two, but still a little bit scruffy. His brown fur was often dotted with mushroom crumbs on his chest and tummy.'

Using this quote and your imagination, draw your own picture of Miika below.